Disney · PIXAR

Cars

Illustrated by
Art Mawhinney and the Disney Storybook Artists

publications international, ltd.

World-famous race car Lightning McQueen has been to many exciting places. But the small town of Radiator Springs is the place he calls home. Cruise around and see if you can spot Lightning's pals:

Mater

Ramone

Fillmore

Lizzie

Guido

Flo

Welcome to Flo's V8 Café, Lightning's favorite place to refuel (literally!) in Radiator Springs. See if you can find these motor-watering morsels:

Ice Cold Coolant

Mouthwatering Motor Oil

transmission fluid

wiper fluid

Anti-Freeze Frosty

car wax

When Lightning needs a tune-up, he heads to Luigi's tire shop. Nobody does tires like Luigi and Guido, and sometimes that means Lightning has to wait his turn! While he's waiting, see if you can spot some of Luigi's favorite tire brands:

Fettuccini Crema

Fettuccini Blanco Maximo

Fettuccini Latte

Gripwell Tires

Tread Star

Wheels-down, Lightning's favorite place in Radiator Springs is Mater's junkyard. That's where Lightning hangs out with his best buddy, Mater! Today, the fast friends are having a junkyard scavenger hunt. Help them find these shiny pieces of junk:

this muffler

this wheel

this tire

this spring

this bumper

this axle

Lightning and Mater go on lots of wild adventures. Sometimes the adventures are so wild (like the time Mater was in a Tokyo drift race) that Lightning doesn't even remember them! Help jog Lightning's memory by searching for these race fans:

this blue car

this purple car

this green car

this pink car

this orange car

this yellow car

Lightning can't quite recall the time he fought bulldozers alongside the great El Materdor, either! Find these red items from the arena to clear up Lightning's foggy memory. *¡Olé!*

this gas can

this poster

beret

Spanish/English dictionary

map of Spain

this sign

The one adventure Lightning will never forget is the time he and Mater stopped an evil spy ring and saved the Queen of England! Good spies like Lightning and Mater notice everything. Can you find these grateful royal guards?

Sure, busting up spy rings is exciting, but for Lightning and Mater, there's no place like home. Today, Lightning is competing in his favorite race—the Radiator Springs Grand Prix. Search the crowd for these souvenirs from Lightning's adventures:

Lightning McQueen bobble-head

PORTO CORSA
sticker

figurine

BIG BENTLEY
poster

Tokyo
road sign

snow globe

Head back to the busy
streets of Radiator Springs
to find these things:

Pull back into Flo's V8 Café
to find as many of these
tasty treats as you can:

☐ 5 cans of oil

☐ 10 cans of lube

☐ 3 cans of grease

☐ 10 cans of wax

☐ 4 boxes of filters

☐ 8 boxes of car soap

Roll back to Luigi's tire shop
and look for these different
racing signs on the wall:

Mosey back to Mater's
junkyard to find these
car parts that are
in the wrong piles:

☐ tire

☐ axle

☐ spring

☐ wheel

☐ muffler

☐ bumper

Race back to Tokyo to look for these colorful elements on the glowing signs:

ビッグ・ラグナット

See if you can spot these British subjects in the crowd at Buckingham Palace:

El Materdor's fans shower him with flowers. Run back to the bullring to find two dozen red roses.

Go back to the Radiator Springs Grand Prix and find these delicious snacks enjoyed by the crowd: